Published by
PEACHTREE PUBLISHERS
1700 Chattahoochee Avenue
Atlanta, Georgia 30318-2112
www.peachtree-online.com

Text and illustrations copyright © 2009 by Sebastien Braun

First published in paperback in Great Britain by HarperCollins Children's Books in 2009
First United States edition published by Peachtree Publishers in 2010
First trade paperback edition published in 2014

illustrations created in india ink, markers, and colored pencil

10 9 8 7 6 5 4 3 (hardcover)
10 9 8 7 6 5 4 3 (trade paperback)

Printed and bound in May 2015 by RR Donnelley in Guangdong Province, China

Library of Congress Cataloging-in-Publication Data

Braun, Sebastien.
Back to bed, Ed! / written and illustrated by Sebastien Braun. — 1st U.S. ed.
p. cm.
Summary: Ed the mouse will not sleep in his own bed, until eventually his exasperated and tired parents find a way to
keep him from joining them in the middle of the night.
iSBN: 978-1-56145-518-8 (hardcover)
iSBN: 978-1-56145-775-5 (trade paperback)
[1. Bedtime—Fiction. 2. Sleep—Fiction. 3. Mice—Fiction.] i. Title.
PZ7.B73779Bac 2010
[E]—dc22
2009024990

# Back to Bed, Ed!

## by Sebastien Braun

PEACHTREE

ATLANTA

Every night Ed loved getting ready for bed.

He played games with Dad,

clip
clop

had a drink,

sip sip

 and cleaned his teeth.

brush
brush

He had a bubbly bath,

**splish**
**splash**

a story with Mom,

then, all tucked in bed,

**kiss kiss**

**night night**

sleep tight!

click

Ed LOVED
going to bed...

but Ed **HATED** staying in bed...

tip toe tip toe...

"Dad! It's too dark in my room."

"Back to bed, Ed," grumbled Dad.

But Ed didn't go back to his bed,

and Dad didn't get much sleep that night.

The next morning Dad said,

"Stay in your own bed, Ed.

You're a BiG mouse now."

But later that night,

tip toe
tip toe

"Mom! There are MONSTERS in my bedroom!"

"Back to bed, Ed," groaned Mom.

But Ed didn't go back to his bed.
Mom and Dad didn't get much sleep that night.

The next morning they slept through the alarm.
Dad was late for work.

Ed was late for preschool.

And so it went on, night after night Ed left his bed.

The next morning they came up with a plan...

That night when Ed went to Mom and Dad's bedroom, the door was shut. He couldn't go in.

Poor Ed didn't know what to do.

sniff
sniff
sniff

Dad came out.

"Come on, Ed, back to bed!" he said.

"The night light is on,
you've got your friend.
There's no need to be scared.
You're a big mouse now."

But Ed didn't stay in bed. He got up and found

 his teddy,

 his frog,

 his duck,

his squirrel.

Now he had all
his little friends
around him.

"There's no need to be scared," he said, "I'm here now."

After that Ed always slept in his own bed,

and everyone got
a good night's sleep...

Well, not quite everyone!

# Sleep tight, Ed!